ADVENTURES OF NIKKI DOG

As Told by Nikki the Dog

WRITTEN BY:
J. MATTHEW NANCE

RESOURCE *Publications* • Eugene, Oregon

Resource Publications
A division of Wipf and Stock Publishers
199 W 8th Ave, Suite 3
Eugene, OR 97401

Adventures of Nikki Dog
As Told by Nikki the Dog
By Nance, J. Matthew
Copyright©2016 by Nance, J. Matthew
ISBN 13: 978-1-5326-8382-4
Publication date 3/4/2019
Previously published by Tate, 2016

A Note to Parents

Now you and your young child can join in the fun with Nikki Dog. Full of both silliness and lessons to learn, *Adventures of Nikki Dog as Told by Nikki the Dog* will have a dog vividly teach your children some of life's basic things such as learning to

- Trust God,

- Be happy with what you already have

- Share with others

- Obey authority

- Stand up to peer pressure

These stories will come to life as your family reads them together. What did everyone like about the story? What did they not like? What can be learned from Nikki? Such discussion, followed by family prayer, will strengthen everyone's walk with God.

Big Green Things

My name is Nikki. When I was just a little puppy, my new master took me on my first walk with him. His big strong arms picked me up, and he put a leash on me. Then he walked out into the big wide world and put me down. I had been out in the big world before, and it had not been kind to me. My little body shook with fear.

As we walked, I kept seeing what looked like big green monsters on the road by every house. I was so scared, I tried to run away and hide, but the leash stopped me. I cried, "Oh, master, one of these monsters is going to eat me!"

Soon, I got too close to one of the big green things and became so afraid I jumped out of my leash and ran straight into one of those monsters, knocking it over. The green thing got down low on its side, opened its mouth, and roared a loud roar. I had never heard anything bark that loud before.

I had no idea that the green monsters were nothing more than trash bins on trash day.

My master ran after me and caught me. He held me until I was no longer afraid. I still do not know what those big green things are, but I know if I stay close to my master, I am not afraid. In my master's arms, I am safe.

I even let my master set me on top of one of the big green monsters. Sitting on top of the monster, I smiled and licked my master's ear. With him, I do not fear the monster.

God says, "Don't be afraid, for I am with you."

—Isaiah 41:10 (NLT)

A Wacky Ride

One day my master took me for a ride in his machine with four round legs. I like sticking my head outside and feeling my ears flap in the wind. On this day, water was falling from the sky, so master would not let me catch the wind.

I had never taken a ride in master's machine when water was falling. Master turned something in front of him, and all of a sudden, it looked like a bird was clearing away the water so we could see better. The bird had long black wings that flapped really close to our faces across something I could see through.

I am the kind of dog that likes to catch birds. I would watch a bird very carefully for a while and then run fast to grab the bird with my mouth.

So I started watching the weird bird. My head went left and right, left and right, moving with the bird, back and forth. Master turned something again, and the bird started cleaning the see-through thing even faster. My head went back and forth even faster.

I had watched the bird long enough. With my whole body, I jumped at the bird. *Bang!* The see-through thing stopped me! I got back in my chair. My head went back and forth, back and forth. After a while, I tried to grab the bird with my paws instead of my mouth. But something stopped me again.

I sat back down and cried. Master told me it was not a bird at all. He said they were something called windshield wipers. Whatever!

Master said, "Oh, Nikki Dog, you have so much already. I feed you and give you all you need. You don't need a bird too. If you go after things you are not meant to have, it will hurt you."

He's right. My nose and paws were hurting the rest of the day from trying to catch that bird.

Be happy with what you have.

—Hebrews 13:5 (GWT)

Getting Adopted into the Royal Family

Can I tell you how I came to be Nikki the Dog? I, Nikki Nikki Dog Dog, am actually a royal dog. I know this to be true because of the way my master loves me. I wasn't born into a royal family though. Master found me and adopted me so I could be in his family.

It all started before I was born. My mommy was not sure who my daddy was. Many people did not like my mommy because she was a pit bull, so she had us pups in the woods. She did the best she could, but one day she left us little ones, rode off in a machine with four round legs, and never came back. I was tired, lonely, and hungry. My brothers and sisters all left me, but I was too afraid to move.

One day the same machine came by, and a man got out. He came into the woods, caught me with a net, and put me in the back of the machine. I hoped to see my mommy, but she wasn't there. The man took me to a cold place with a hard floor and lots of barking dogs. Someone came and fed me and sprayed me with water, but there was no love.

Then one day, a very caring person came to see me. He signed some papers to take me with him. He is now my master. Master adopted me, and I am his forever. I am happy because master does what is best for me.

Master doesn't spray me with water. He uses his hands to clean me, and I hold my head high.

I know I am a royal dog because of the way master calls my name. He says with a very happy voice, "Nikki Nikki Dog Dog!" I love hearing him call my name. When he does, I run to him. Then my body starts spinning around and around as I do the dance of joy for the master. Do you belong to the good master like I do? Have you become a part of the royal family?

He adopted you as His own.

—Romans 8:15 (NLT)

Learning to Share

I often took my master out for a walk. One day we came to the place where he would give me a treat. As always he pulled a treat out of his pocket, dusted it off, and waited for me to sit. As soon as I did, he gave me the treat. I was happy with what he gave me until he pulled out another treat but did not give it to *me*.

Master walked over to a little broken-down shack. There was a wet nose sticking out between two boards. I watched as master gave *my* treat to *that* dog!

I was mad. I barked at the dog, but he did not give me my treat. I growled.

When we got home, I scolded master for what he had done. In my most pitiful bark, I said, "Am I not a royal dog? All those treats are mine! Only mine!"

Master took me in his arms and said, "Nikki Nikki Dog Dog, you once were homeless like that mutt. I took you in and cared for you. What if no one had cared for *you*? I have plenty of love for both you *and* that other dog."

The next time we went on a walk and came to the spot where I always got a treat, master pulled *two* treats out and dusted them off. He looked at me, and then he looked at the wet nose sticking out of the shack. Master looked back at me for a long time without saying anything. I knew what he wanted me to do. When I sat my bottom down, master gave me a treat. I took the treat over to the poor dog and sat with the dog while *he* ate the treat. Then I licked his fur clean.

I was so happy caring for that dog, I forgot all about my own treat. I asked master if we could make the dog a part of our royal family. So master brought that cute mutt home with us. He is now my brother. He is big and black, so we call him Bear Dog. I enjoy sharing things with Bear Dog. Bear and I are planning a dog party for all the dogs in Bear's old hood. At the party, we will give away all our master's treats. He won't mind!

I like to share and care. It's what I should do as a part of the royal family.

Be generous and ready to share.

—1 Timothy 6:18 (NASV)

Running Away from Home

When Bear Dog came to live with us, he didn't think I was fun since I was small. As I grew, Bear decided he *liked* to play with me.

Early one morning Bear dug under the fence and crawled out into the big world. He barked for me to come. I looked at the hole under the fence, and then I looked back to the door where master comes out to feed me and love me. My head went this way and that way, back and forth between go and stay.

I wanted Bear to think I was fun. So I crawled under the fence. Bear and I took off running. We crossed a big highway, and lots of machines with round legs made screeching sounds with their legs. I don't know why.

We smelled water and followed our noses. At the lake, there was a black animal that was not happy to see us. He turned his rear toward us, raised his white tail, and sprayed the most awful smell at us.

Bear and I jumped in the lake to get rid of the smell, but the water was frozen. All of a sudden, the ice began to crack and we fell down into the cold water. When we finally got back to land, the wind was blowing and the water on my fur froze.

My ears perked up! It was master's voice! I sniffed the air. I smelled master! The wind blew again, and I couldn't smell him. I was mad at Bear for leading me away from home. My belly was empty, and the grass burrs sticking to the ice on my body hurt. I started to cry.

Bear dog wanted me to keep following him. I did *not* want to follow Bear any more, so he ran off. My best friend had led me to a bad place. Then he left me all alone, cold and hungry. Some friend! If I had not followed Bear, I would have been eating breakfast at home. I had made a bad choice.

I heard people coming, so I hid in the bushes. People were mean to me when I was a little puppy. Under the bushes, I found mushrooms to eat but they made my tummy hurt and I threw up.

Oh, if I would have just stayed at home! What I thought would be great fun in the big world just ended up hurting me. I thought my friend would only do what was good for me, but I was wrong. I missed my master so much!

I was very tired and fell asleep under the bushes. I thought I was dreaming when I heard the squeak of master's left running shoe. My ears perked up. It was no dream. I heard him running toward me. He called my name loud and clear, "Nikki Nikki Dog Dog!" Master ran right to me, pulled me out from under the bushes, and held me in his arms. I was so happy! I licked his face and ears. Even though I had run away from home, my master was not mad at me. He was so happy to find me.

His father said, "This son of mine was...lost, but now he is found." So the party began.

—Luke 15:22-24 (NLT)